Zack's Zippers

The Sound of Z

by Cecilia Minden and Joanne Meier · illustrated by Bob Ostrom

The Child's World

Published by The Child's World®
1980 Lookout Drive
Mankato, MN 56003-1705
800-599-READ
www.childsworld.com

The Child's World®: Mary Berendes, Publishing Director
The Design Lab: Design and page production

Library of Congress Cataloging-in-Publication Data
Minden, Cecilia.
  Zack's zippers : the sound of Z / by Cecilia Minden
and Joanne Meier ; illustrated by Bob Ostrom.
    p. cm.
  ISBN 978-1-60253-424-7 (library bound : alk. paper)
  1. English language—Consonants—Juvenile literature.
2. English language—Phonetics—Juvenile literature. 3.
Reading—Phonetic method—Juvenile literature. I. Meier,
Joanne D. II. Ostrom, Bob. III. Title.
  PE1159.M578 2010
  [E]—dc22   2010005613

Printed in the United States of America in Mankato, MN.
July 2010
F11538

NOTE TO PARENTS AND EDUCATORS:

The Child's World® has created this series with the goal of exposing children to engaging stories and illustrations that assist in phonics development. The books in the series will help children learn the relationships between the letters of written language and the individual sounds of spoken language. This contact helps children learn to use these relationships to read and write words.

The books in this series follow a similar format. An introductory page, to be read by an adult, introduces the child to the phonics feature, or sound, that will be highlighted in the book. Read this page to the child, stressing the phonic feature. Help the student learn how to form the sound with her mouth. The story and engaging illustrations follow the introduction. At the end of the story, word lists categorize the feature words into their phonic elements.

Each book in this series has been carefully written to meet specific readability requirements. Close attention has been paid to elements such as word count, sentence length, and vocabulary. Readability formulas measure the ease with which the text can be read and understood. Each book in this series has been analyzed using the Spache readability formula.

Reading research suggests that systematic phonics instruction can greatly improve students' word recognition, spelling, and comprehension skills. This series assists in the teaching of phonics by providing students with important opportunities to apply their knowledge of phonics as they read words, sentences, and text.

This is the letter z.

In this book, you will read words
that have the **z** sound as in:
zipper, zebra, and *zoo.*

This is Zack.

Zack likes zippers.

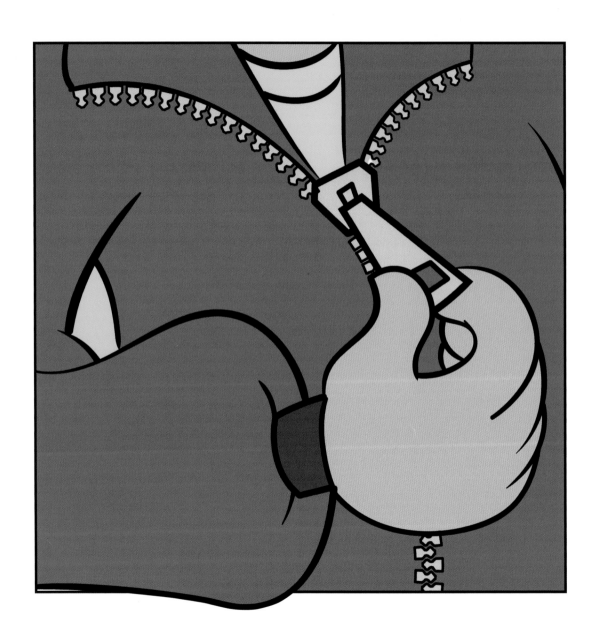

Zack likes big zippers.

Zack's coat has a big zipper.

Zack likes little zippers.

Zack's pocket has a

little zipper.

Zack looks in his pocket.

What is in Zack's pocket?

14

There is a toy zebra.

Zack looks in his other pocket.

What is in the pocket?

There is a ticket in
Zack's pocket.

It is a ticket to the zoo!

"I hope I see a real zebra

at the zoo," says Zack.

Fun Facts

Did you know there are three kinds of zebras living in Africa? Africa is the only continent where you can find zebras living in the wild. Not all zebras look exactly alike. Some may have slightly different coloring or stripe patterns. Zebras always travel together in herds. One male zebra called a *stallion*, several mothers, and their young make up a family herd. Until young male zebras can create their own family herds, they travel in herds with other young males.

The Berlin Zoo in Germany, the Bronx Zoo in New York, and the San Diego Zoo in California are the world's largest zoos. Many people consider the Vienna Zoo in Austria to be the world's oldest zoo. It opened in 1752. There are approximately 1,500 zoos worldwide.

Activity

Learning the Different Ways Zippers Are Used
Look around your home to discover all the ways zippers are used. Of course, you will check the coat closet. Don't forget to look in the laundry room. Maybe there is a laundry bag with a zipper on it. Check all over the house and make a list. Have your family guess how many different ways zippers are used in your home. You will probably surprise them when you share your list.

To Learn More

Books
About the Sound of Z
Moncure, Jane Belk. *My "z" Sound Box®*. Mankato, MN: The Child's World, 2009.

About Zebras
Fontes, Justine, Ron Fontes, and Peter Grosshauser (illustrator). *How the Zebra Got Its Stripes*. New York: Golden Books, 2002.
Fredericks, Anthony D., and Gerry Ellis (photographer). *Zebras*. Minneapolis, MN: Lerner Publications Co., 2001.
Reitano, John, and William Haines (illustrator). *What If The Zebras Lost Their Stripes?* New York: Paulist Press, 1998.

About Zippers
Butterfield, Moira, and Peter Utton et al. *Zippers, Buttons, and Bows*. Hauppauge, NY: Barron's Educational Series, 2000.
Pulver, Robin, and R. W. Alley (illustrator). *Mrs. Toggle's Zipper*. Aladdin Books, 1993.

About Zoos
Harrison, Sarah. *A Day at a Zoo*. Minneapolis, MN: Millbrook Press, 2009.
Komiya, Teruyuki, Kristin Earhart, and Toyofumi Fukuda (photographer). *Life-Size Zoo*. New York: Seven Footer Kids, 2009.

Web Sites
Visit our home page for lots of links about the Sound of Z:
childsworld.com/links

Note to Parents, Teachers, and Librarians: We routinely check our Web links to make sure they're safe, active sites—so encourage your readers to check them out!

Z Feature Words

Proper Names
Zack

**Feature Words in
Initial Position**
zebra
zipper
zoo

About the Authors

Cecilia Minden, PhD, is the former director
of the Language and Literacy Program at
the Harvard Graduate School of Education.
She is now a reading consultant for school
and library publications. She earned her
PhD in reading education from the University
of Virginia. Cecilia and her husband, Dave
Cupp, live outside Chapel Hill, North
Carolina. They enjoy sharing their love of
reading with their grandchildren, Chelsea
and Qadir.

Joanne Meier, PhD, has worked as an
elementary school teacher, university
professor, and researcher. She earned her
BA in early childhood education from the
University of South Carolina, and her MEd
and PhD in education from the University
of Virginia. She currently works as a
literacy consultant for schools and private
organizations. Joanne lives in Virginia with her
husband Eric, daughters Kella and Erin, two
cats, and a gerbil.

About the Illustrator

Bob Ostrom has been illustrating children's
books for nearly twenty years. A graduate of
the New England School of Art & Design at
Suffolk University, Bob has worked for such
companies as Disney, Nickelodeon, and
Cartoon Network. He lives in North Carolina
with his wife Melissa and three children, Will,
Charlie, and Mae.